THE
MYSTERY
OF THE
SCHOOL
ON FIRE

First published in India in 2020 by HarperCollins Children's Books
An imprint of HarperCollins *Publishers*
A-75, Sector 57, Noida, Uttar Pradesh 201301, India
www.harpercollins.co.in

2 4 6 8 10 9 7 5 3 1

Text © Ravi Subramanian 2020
Illustrations © HarperCollins *Publishers* India 2020

P-ISBN: 978-93-5357-931-9
E-ISBN: 978-93-5357-932-6

Designed in 11 pt/ 15 Archer by Isha Nagar

Printed and bound at Replika Press Pvt. Ltd.

THE
SMS
DETECTIVE
AGENCY
Book 1

THE
MYSTERY
OF THE
SCHOOL
ON FIRE

RAVI SUBRAMANIAN

Illustrated by
Ayeshe Sadr and Ishaan Dasgupta

HarperCollins*Children's Books*

INTRODUCTION

Introducing the stars of this book – nine-year-old twins, Aditya and Akriti and their best friend, Kabir. Although the three are very good friends, they are also very different. Aditya, by virtue of being born a couple of minutes before Akriti, is the elder of the twins. A tall boy, almost a five-footer, **Aditya** always finds himself standing at the back of the class, owing to his height. He is the Dude in the group.

Unlike Aditya, **Kabir** is a lazy kid. He is someone who prefers to be a goalie in a game of football. When leaning on the goal post, he always hopes that the ball stays on the other side of the ground. A large frame sitting on his nose makes him look studious, though he is quite the opposite. He is the Nerd of the gang, simply because he looks like one.

Akriti is the smartest of the lot. Someone who always knows how important it is to listen to the other person, Akriti is smarter than both Aditya and Kabir. Her general awareness and knowledge is far higher than the other two. It is not without reason that she is the Genius of the group.

The three are Fourth Graders at Sacred Heart Public School, one of the oldest and most renowned schools in Solan.

Although they secretly think they are D'N'G meaning Dude, Nerd and Genius, they call themselves the Super Mystery Solvers or ...
(TURN THE PAGE TO FIND OUT!)

THE SMS GANG

CHAPTER 1

The Fourth Graders of Sacred Heart Public School were on a visit to the local post office in Solan. Solan was a small picturesque town at the foothills of the Himalayas. It was a town where gossip spread quickly and nothing—absolutely nothing—remained hidden. A place where crime was unknown till a few years ago. So much so that lack of work had made the city police rusty and lethargic.

Since Solan was in a valley, the mornings and evenings could get quite cold. But not today. Today was unusually warm. The sun was at its brightest.

Aditya was the first to take off the red sweater that was part of the school uniform and tie it around his waist. His classmates were quick to follow.

Fortunately for the children, Sister Maria Leena, the school principal, did not notice this as she and the Postmaster General of Solan were walking a few steps ahead of the students.

Sister Maria Leena was a stickler for discipline. She had been the principal of Sacred Heart for as long as one could remember. In fact, almost every family in Solan had been through the portals of her school at some point or the other.

The post office was an imposing brick structure set in the middle of Solan. Legend had it that during the freedom struggle, it was the place where the local freedom fighters would meet and draw up plans to fight the British. Spread over a large parcel of land, it was one of the oldest and prettiest buildings in Solan. Though emails and telephone calls had taken over, a visit to the Solan post office was an annual trek for the Fourth and Fifth Graders at all schools in Solan.

As they approached the imposing structure, the postmaster

pointed towards a small pebbled pathway that led towards the side of the building. 'The mail sorting room is to the right,' he said. 'This is where letters are sorted area-wise, for delivery.'

'No one writes letters these days,' the postmaster complained to Sister Leena. He had been the postmaster long enough to see changes not just within his building but in the town as well. 'Couriers and emails have taken over.' Although they were speaking in hushed tones, Aditya, who was in the bunch of kids right behind them, was close enough to hear their lament. Aditya of the popular Kapoor twin duo was, for a change, standing ahead of all the other kids, a privilege he otherwise never got, because of his height. Curious to hear what was being said, he nudged his way ahead to listen in on the conversation. 'I am not surprised,' Sister Leena said, shrugging her shoulders. 'Something like that is happening to us too. Look at the new school that has opened down in the valley.'

'Which one? Solan International School?' The postmaster asked, moving his hand through his mop of grey hair.
'SIS,' Sister Leena corrected him. 'It is S.I.S, not Solan International School.'

She frowned and rolled her eyes. 'SIS sounds cool. Doesn't it? New building, modern amenities. They are paying more money to teachers and weaning them away from our school,' she said sadly. 'The old order changeth, yielding place to the new.' 'Yours is definitely a better school,' the postmaster said, trying to cheer her up. 'You don't need to worry.'

'We know that, the students know that, but somehow the coolness quotient of the new school is so much higher,' she sighed.

'And who doesn't want to be cool these days,' the postmaster nodded, completing what Sister Leena wanted to say. 'Exactly,' Sister Leena found herself rolling her eyes again. 'I mustn't do that too often! How will I tell the students to stop rolling their eyes if I get better at it than them,' she thought, shaking her head. 'We have a school inspection coming up. The inspection will decide which is a better school. Ours or the new one. Let's see.'

Aditya was sad to hear his principal feel uncertain about the school's future. Truth be told, even his parents had discussed shifting him and his twin sister Akriti to the new school. Happily, it had remained just a discussion. The twins had protested so wildly to the suggestion that their parents had to relent. 'We love Sister Leena, our teachers, our friends! How can you think of moving us to another school?' they had cried, mirroring each other's expressions perfectly.

As the postmaster led Sister Leena into the building, he asked, 'When is the inspection?'
'Friday,' Sister Leena replied.

'Four days to go,' the postmaster said. 'Knowing you, I am sure you will be fully prepared.'

'Oh yes!' Sister Leena's face lit up. 'We do this every year. It is now a complete and thorough exercise. We paint the school. Refurbish the classrooms and labs. Train the students.' Then she smiled and added, 'We will come out on top. Lots of effort has gone into it.'

'I am sure you will,' the postmaster smiled reassuringly as they entered the mail sorting room on the far left of the post office complex.

Suddenly, the quiet mail sorting room was filled with the sound of choral music. Sister Leena quickly pulled out her phone from the pocket of her habit.

'Call from school,' she said as she lifted the phone to her ear, walking away from the crowd. By this time all

the other children and the rest of the teachers had also collected in the mail sorting room and were surprised to see Sister Leena rushing out of the room.
Within a few minutes a very agitated looking Sister Leena returned. Her face was a deep red, and droplets of sweat were streaming down her sideburns. 'I am extremely sorry. I will have to rush,' she said to the postmaster.

'Is everything OK?' the postmaster asked, with a look of concern on his face.

'There has been a fire on the school premises.'

A collective gasp went up in the air.

'In the science lab,' Sister Leena muttered as she hurriedly left the room.

CHAPTER 2

Fortunately, the fire incident in the science lab had been a small one. A bunch of papers kept on the table had caught fire. Since the table was next to the window, the fire had spread to the curtains, leading to panic. Luckily for the school, the fire had been contained before it could spread beyond the curtains.

For Sister Leena there was nothing more important than the school and nothing of greater concern than the safety of her students. In fact, whenever the children went for a trek on the hillside she checked each bag herself and made sure it contained a small torch—even though it was a day trek—an umbrella, strong cord for climbing and a water bottle. It only takes one mishap to change the life of a person, she would argue. Which was why she was very disturbed by the fire. She was also worried that they were only four days away from the school inspection and instances like this would lead to uncomfortable questions.

By the time Aditya, Akriti and the rest of the class got back from the post office excursion, things had settled down. A bright red truck from the Solan Fire Department stood on the school ground. As the Fourth Graders went up to their class, they could see a big huddle in Sister Leena's office. Three men were bent over Sister Leena's table engaged in a serious discussion. Aditya could make out from their uniform that they were from the local fire department. Rehamat Chacha, the school peon, was serving tea in plastic cups.

The police chief of Solan, Chief Walia was also there. The twins knew him because his son, Kabir the Nerd, was also in the same class as Aditya and Akriti.

Chief Walia was also the head of the School PTA (the Parent Teacher Association).

The rest of the day was like any other. A bored Aditya was poring over the maths sums that the class had been asked to solve, when a crumpled piece of paper landed on his table. When he turned to see where it was coming from, he caught sight of Kabir with a wide grin on his face. After making sure that the teacher was not looking his way, he opened the chit and spread it out in front of him.

'Meet me in the washroom,' it said. He recognized Kabir's handwriting.

Aditya turned and looked at Kabir again. He could see that Kabir was desperate to tell him something. But, before Aditya could say anything, Kabir got up from his seat and walked to the maths teacher, sought her permission to leave and walked out to the washroom. Aditya followed suit. Both boys

raced down the corridor, their footsteps echoing off the old stone walls.

'Adiii!' Kabir ran towards him the moment Aditya entered the washroom. 'You know dude, the fire in the lab was not an accident.'

'What?' Aditya stopped short, stunned. He looked around hurriedly to make sure no one was around. 'Are you out of your mind, Kabir?'

'I might be. But Dad surely isn't,' Kabir responded. 'Apparently, the place where the fire started does not have any electrical wires. It was close to the window. So how did the fire start? Dude, the fire didn't start off accidentally,' Kabir declared with a sense of finality.

'What? What are you saying?' Aditya said as they slowly started walking back to the classroom. He couldn't hold back his excitement. 'Are you hinting that someone started the fire,' adding after a long pause, 'intentionally?'

Kabir looked at him, eyes round with excitement and eyebrows raised. Aditya took that as an affirmative.

'Your Dad told you this?' he asked.
'Why else would I be so confident? I rushed back to the classroom to tell you and Akriti, but the teacher had already come in.'
'But why would someone try to harm the school? Why would someone try to set fire to the lab?'

'Sister Leena is sure of sabotage. She feels that the person who did this wanted to harm the reputation of the school. Everyone knows about Friday's inspection. A fire accident in a school just before an inspection would be a disaster.'

'Are you saying that whoever set fire to the lab, didn't want the school to clear the inspection?'

'That, you go figure out,' Kabir said, through glasses that had steamed up in the excitement. He now took them off and started rubbing them vigorously.

'Why me? Aren't we the SMS gang – you, me and Akriti?' Aditya struck a note of camaraderie. 'We will figure out who is trying to defame the school.' He brought his palm up and gave Kabir a high five. 'Let's go.'

CHAPTER 3

'See, this is why I wanted you to shift the kids to the new school.' Akriti's ears perked up when she came out of the shower the next morning, and heard her grandfather talking to her mother. She walked closer to the door and peeped out only to see him wave the morning newspaper at her Mom and repeat what he had just said. It was unusual to see her Grandpa at this time. He normally came out of his bedroom only after he had read the morning newspaper end to end. But today appeared to be different. He seemed agitated as he stood next to the dining table talking to Mom and towering over Dad who sat there eating his breakfast. Grandpa turned to look at Dad through his thick glasses a couple of times, but Dad continued to eat quietly and did not say anything in response. Grandpa would always choose the wrong time to have the most intense conversations. Whenever he had these conversations, his face would shake angrily and the flowy white hair on his head would move in sync.

'What can I do when the kids don't want to shift?' their Mom asked, trying to keep calm. 'Kids these days have a mind of their own. You can't force them to accept your decisions.'

Worried that the conversation with Grandpa would upset Mom, Dad hurriedly entered the conversation. 'Talk to them. Convince them,' he said as he pushed his chair back and got up from the table. The breakfast of rava upma was over. 'I am getting late for work,' he declared, as he grabbed his coat and walked out of the house. Dad was a banker. His bank opened its branch at 9.00 a.m., but he was usually in office by 8.45 a.m.

Akriti sneaked up to the table in the living room and looked at the newspaper that her grandfather had dumped there. What she saw made her eyes go red with anger. She snatched the paper and rushed back to her room where Aditya was busy getting ready for school.

'Adi,' she said loudly as she spread out the newspaper on the bed in front of him.

'Close Shave for 400 Students. Fire in Science Lab of Sacred Heart Public School,' screamed a headline from the front page of the newspaper.

Aditya stared at the newspaper, blood rushing to his cheeks. He was angry. It was not the news article that had caught his attention. What peeved both Aditya and Akriti was that right next to the news article was an advertisement, covering half the page. For Solan International School. That too with a cheeky tagline: *We only fire up your child's imagination. Nothing else.*

'How dare they do this?' Akriti thumped the table with her right hand. Funnily, the twins looked most like each other when they were angry! And as they stared together at the newspaper, their faces turned a deep crimson. 'Looks like these guys want to sabotage the reputation of our school? Why else would they put out this "FIRE UP" ad?'

Aditya's eyes grew round and big. 'Akriti,' he

whispered, 'could these SIS guys be behind the fire in the lab?'

'I am not so sure!' Then hearing their mother's voice, they both turned towards the door. Their Mom had heard their conversation as she entered the room. She was carrying two platefuls of sandwiches for them. The twins adored their Mom. It was amazing how she managed to remain calm and unruffled always. She also liked to explain things they didn't understand and seldom got angry with them.

Even today, she had barely heard their conversation when she started to explain. 'Such large front-page advertisements are booked

days in advance. So they couldn't have put out the ad yesterday, after the fire. That said, the tagline could surely not have been a coincidence. They would have created the tagline only yesterday. After the fire. If that's what they did, they are not legally wrong, but then morally ...' And here she paused. 'Morally they may have just gone over the line.' Then as she turned to walk away, she added, 'I have friends in the newspaper office. Let me check with them.'

'Thanks, Mom,' Aditya smiled. Then turning towards Akriti who was almost ready to leave for school, he said, 'But, even if Solan International was responsible for the fire, how did they manage? The science lab is on the third floor. The same as our classroom. Away from the main gate. It is almost impossible for someone to sneak up unnoticed, set fire to the lab and escape.'

'Correct,' Akriti agreed. 'Impossible for someone from outside to do this. So Solan International School couldn't have orchestrated this,' she added, with a note of alarm in her voice.

'Unless …' Aditya said, walking towards Akriti.
'Unless?' Akriti queried. She knew what Aditya was getting at, but wanted him to say it.

'Unless there is an insider helping them.'

Akriti banged her fist on the table in anger.
'Damn,' she said. 'Who could it be?'

Chapter 4

The twins were running late. As they rushed into class, Kabir came forward to meet them. 'You saw the papers today?' he asked excitedly. And without waiting for either of them to respond, he added, 'Are you also thinking what I am?'

Aditya didn't say anything. He quietly walked to his desk and plonked down his stuffed backpack. Then he sat down and closed his eyes and began to think. He tried to imagine what could have happened in the science lab that day. After a couple of minutes, he opened his eyes and looked at Akriti. 'The person

who did this would have been in the vicinity
of the lab. He would have had to be in the lab to set
fire to the papers there. Someone would have seen
him.' Then he looked at Kabir and asked, 'Do the cops
suspect anyone?'

'They have one lead. And that too seems a far-fetched
one,' Kabir replied.
'Who?' Akriti asked. 'Who do they suspect?'
'Rehamat Chacha!' Kabir rolled his eyes.
'Are you serious!' Akriti groaned. 'It's impossible! He
has been around from the time Mom was a student
here. She has told us stories of how protective he was
towards children. He has spent his life in this school
ringing the school bell, managing traffic outside the
school and making sure kids are safe. He would never
do anything to harm kids.'

'Well, Dad said that he is the only one who seems to
have a motive.'
'What motive? I don't believe that he would have done
anything like that,' Aditya shot back at Kabir. The
soft-spoken, gaunt Rehamat Chacha was everyone's
favourite. Always dressed in light coloured pathan

suits, he was as familiar a part of the school as the building itself. To suggest that he could have attempted to set fire to the lab when the children were in school was unthinkable.

'I don't want to believe it either. But everything seems stacked against him. He was the last person to be seen coming out of the lab. The cleaners saw him come out minutes before the fire was noticed,' Kabir reasoned. 'While I was waiting for Dad outside the principal's office, I heard some teachers talk about how Sister Leena had yelled at Rehamat Chacha a few days back. When you consider that fact, you get the motive you were looking for. Don't you?'

'You don't set fire to your own house because you had an argument. Do you?' Akriti came to Rehamat Chacha's defence. 'I find the suggestion outlandish. Just because ...'
'Driinggggggg.' The school bell cut short their discussion.

'Well, if you want to save him then you better figure out what happened,' Kabir declared. 'As of now, he

40

seems to be the only suspect.' Saying this, he walked towards his seat at the far end of the classroom.

So began another day at school. Akriti felt restless. 'Was Rehamat Chacha really guilty? Would he go against the school which had been his home for the last two decades, maybe more?' She shook her head and looked up. The entire class was standing. 'Good Morning, Sir,' echoed in the classroom. She stood up quickly, smoothing out the creases in her uniform.

'Students,' Pandey Sir, the science teacher addressed them. Although Pandey Sir was a science teacher there was something completely unscientific about his looks. The hair on his head stood up straight, at a gravity defying angle, and how he managed to lean on the table without his belly rolling off his legs, was a mystery. Akriti was not interested in what he was going to say. She turned to look out of the window. From where she was sitting, she could look straight into the science lab. Akriti saw a visibly worried Sister Maria Leena standing outside the lab talking to a few

teachers. Rehamat Chacha was standing at the far
end of the corridor. His long face said it all. He looked
upset, as anyone would be in such a situation.
Akriti was so lost in thought that she didn't hear
her name being called out. And it was only when
the classmate sitting next to her poked her with her
pencil, that she jumped back to attention.

'Anything wrong, Akriti?' Pandey Sir's voice rang in
her ears.

'No, Sir. Nothing,' she mumbled as she hurriedly opened
her notebook and looked at the science teacher.
Pandey Sir smiled. 'I know what is going through your
mind. Yesterday's incident is bothering all of you.
Don't worry. It was a small fire, thankfully. I hope the
School Inspectors don't make an issue of this.'
'It is already in the papers, Sir,' Kabir said.

'Yes, I know.' Pandey Sir agreed. 'Very unfortunate that
this has happened in my lab, that too during my last
week here.'

A hush descended on the classroom. A question escaped Akriti's lips. 'Last week, Sir?' Aditya jerked his head back towards Akriti.

'Yes,' Pandey Sir continued. 'I am moving on. This is my last week here. Sister Leena requested me to stay back till the inspection was over.'

No one spoke for a while. Finally, one student gathered the courage to stand up and ask, 'Are you moving out of Solan, Sir?'

'No, my dear. I am moving to Solan. I am joining SIS. I will not be here, but if any of you want to meet me outside school, I will be very happy to help.'

Pandey Sir was the first high profile teacher to be exiting Sacred Heart to join Solan International. A few teachers had already left, but Pandey Sir was the most prominent of them all. None of the other teachers was as popular as Pandey Sir. Sister Leena's worst fears were coming true. But that was not what was bothering Aditya. When he again craned his neck and turned back to look at Akriti, he found her also deep in thought. Aditya took out a piece of paper and started scribbling. Once done, he rolled it up and lobbed it towards Akriti. He saw her reach out and grab the paper ball in mid-flight. Her eyes lit up when she opened it and spread it out on the table.

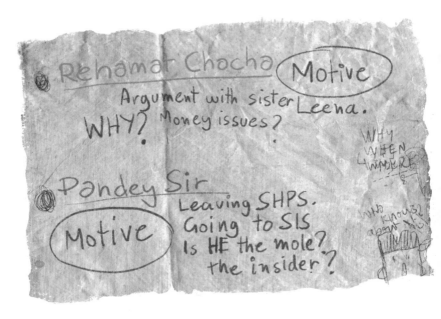

And when she nodded her head after reading it, he knew they were on the right path. And even if they weren't, they were at least thinking along similar lines.

CHAPTER 5

'Rehamat Chacha,' Akriti called out when she saw him coming down the corridor after ringing the school bell. Akriti was on her way back from the school office where she had gone to hand over a letter from her father's bank supporting a sponsorship request.

Rehamat Chacha was walking down the steps that led through the garden to the main school gate. He was headed towards his favourite spot near the gate. It was a place from where he could look up at the school and keep an eye on everything that was going on. A smile lit up his face when he saw Akriti running towards him.

Chacha gently placed his palm on her head. Akriti wanted to ask him a thousand questions, but didn't know where to begin. 'How are you, Rehamat Chacha?' she asked, 'You look tired.'

'I am fine, my dear. Just too much work. You know the school inspection is two days away. Lots of cleaning work to do. The school has to be decked up. You know how important it is for us to clear this inspection. For the first time, we have competition from SIS. We have to teach them a lesson. We have class, my child. We have class. They have glamour. But we have class.'

'Then why are our teachers leaving and going there?'
'Who is leaving?' Rehamat Chacha asked.
'Pandey Sir. He told all of us yesterday that he is leaving.'

'Oh, Pandey Sir. That's a long story.' Rehamat Chacha sighed. 'I have seen so many science teachers come and go. But haven't seen anyone like him. He is very good. Very unfortunate that the fire happened in his lab.'

'What actually happened? Everyone is saying that you were the last person to come out of the lab before the fire began.'

'Yes, my child. I was the last one to come out. Pandey Sir had noticed some water leakage in the lab and asked me to shift some equipment so that it didn't get damaged. I shifted the equipment closer to the window, away from the water pipe. I then cleaned the entire lab. I even opened the curtains to let the sunlight in, so that the dampness would go away. Pandey Sir was also there with me. After he left, I just cleaned up the rest of the mess and walked out of the lab. Within minutes of our leaving the lab, the fire started. I don't know how it happened.'

Akriti didn't probe further. She didn't want to

embarrass Rehamat Chacha. 'Is the lab back in shape, Chacha?' she asked.

Rehamat Chacha nodded his head. 'I was here till late last night. We had to fix it. Couldn't even go to meet my son in the hospital.'

Akriti looked up. 'Hospital?' she asked, alarmed. 'Why

is your son in hospital?'

'Malaria. In fact, he has been in hospital since the last four days. Because of the inspection I didn't even take a day off to go be with him.'

'I hope he recovers quickly, Chacha,' Akriti said, before

rushing back to Aditya and Kabir.

'It could be Rehamat Chacha,' she announced when she was sure no one was within earshot. 'His son is in hospital. He needs money. He was the last person seen coming out of the lab.' She gave them a rundown on her conversation with Rehamat Chacha. Kabir and Aditya listened carefully.

'A person in that position, could have schemed against the school, to make a quick buck,' Aditya inferred, then added wisely, 'when it comes down to one's family, people are willing to do anything.'

'That leaves us with two suspects,' Kabir said. 'Chacha and ...'

'Pandey Sir,' the three of them exclaimed in unison.

CHAPTER 6

'Adi! Adi! Adi!' Kabir came screaming towards the twins as they sat having lunch. The school lunch room was a cacophony of sound with several students slouched over each table. It was as if the entire school had descended there.

Aditya and Akriti were seated on the most coveted stools in the pantry room – the stools that overlooked the valley. From this height, Aditya could see their home and the houses that lined the street. The roadside Kirana store marked the end of the lane, beyond which he could see the grassy hillside.

The sight was so magical – like a poster they would never tire of.

'Adi. Akri.' Kabir was now standing next to them and yelling in their ears.

'Why are you panting like this? Take a deep breath, have some water.' Akriti reached out for her water bottle, much to Aditya's displeasure. 'Why do you always mother everyone?' he asked, rolling his eyes so hard that Kabir thought that he would have seen his own brain.

'Forget that,' Kabir panted. He then looked around to see if there was anyone paying attention to what they were saying.

Aditya looked down at Kabir's trousers. They were wet. 'You peed your pants?' he asked Kabir with a weird expression on his face, before throwing back his head and laughing wildly.

'Oh, shut up.' Akriti stepped into the conversation. 'Don't be gross.'

'No. No. Wait till you hear what I heard,' Kabir said in hushed tones.

'We have been waiting from the time you ran in, after having peed your pants.' Aditya was finding it hard to stop laughing.

'I was in the bathroom. The door was closed. There was no one else there. And then guess who walked in?'

'Who?' both Aditya and Akriti asked together.

Kabir brought his hands up to his head and made the horns of a devil. 'Paaandey Siiiirrr,' he said in a gruff voice.

'So what? Pandey Sir is human. I'm sure he has to pee,' Aditya said, before looking at Akriti and starting to laugh again.

'Of course, he does.' Kabir said crossly. 'But the strange thing is, he hadn't come to the toilet to pee or poop.'

'Then?'

'He was on his phone. He didn't hear me in the washroom. So he presumed he was alone.'

'Will you stop telling the story in bits and pieces.' Akriti was getting both excited and angry.

Kabir knew he was in control, and was enjoying every moment of it. 'Have some patience, Akriti. And you know what ...' he paused to build up the twins' interest. 'Even though he thought he was alone, he was still whispering into the phone.'

'Who was he talking to?' Aditya said loudly. Then noticing some children on the next table looking towards them, he quickly picked up his sandwich and took a large bite.

'Don't know,' Kabir said. 'But he was talking about money. He was telling someone that he has not got his money. He said, "I have finished my work. You need to make sure you make the full payment soon. And no, not cheque. I need cash. I have delivered the result you wanted."'

Aditya and Akriti were both surprised and excited to hear this. 'This can only mean that he is asking for money for a job done. Do you think he could be asking for payment for having set fire to the science lab,' Akriti said in a low voice.

'He didn't exactly set fire to the science lab,' Kabir answered.

'Whatever!' Akriti said.

'More importantly, why was he whispering into the

phone? Had he done something illegal? Something for which he was so ashamed he had to go to the toilet to speak!'

'So did Pandey Sir get his money?' Akriti was getting restless.

'If you guys allow me to speak then I will tell you. Otherwise don't blame me if my memory fails me.'
'Oh, come on,' Aditya implored. 'Stop acting pricey.'
'OK.' There was a gleam in Kabir's eye. 'Pandey Sir is going this evening to collect his cash.'
'Today? Where? What time?' Akriti fired off questions in one go.

'After school. He is going after school today to collect his cash.'

CHAPTER 7

That evening, Aditya and Kabir stood in the lane
adjacent to a large bungalow in one of Solan's most
scenic locations. They were waiting for Pandey Sir to
emerge from the bungalow's big iron gates. Kabir and
Aditya had followed Pandey Sir after school, to find
out who he was meeting to collect his money.

Pandey Sir had left school at 4.00 p.m. He had walked
a mile and a half down a long winding road towards
the valley, before turning right into a narrow private
lane. A lane which led to the bungalow with ten foot-
high iron gates. Kabir and Aditya had managed to

remain hidden as they trailed him from school. Aditya was huffing and panting by the time they settled down on a spot twenty yards from the gate.

They waited for over an hour, but nothing happened. It was beginning to get dark. In these parts, the sun set early. Aditya was getting worried. He had to get back home on time. He had bunked his special classes to follow Pandey Sir. Akriti had promised to cover up for him at home.

'We need to go back,' he whispered to Kabir.

'Let's wait for some more time. We don't even know whose house this is. The name plate can't be seen from here.'

'Five minutes. After which we have to go. We will come back later,' Aditya pleaded. He was getting more anxious by the minute.

'OK, tell you what. You wait here,' Kabir said. 'I will casually walk up to the gate, see whose house this is and then we will leave.' He was confident that in case he got into trouble, his father would rescue him. 'We can't come this far and go back without knowing whose house Pandey Sir has walked into to collect cash.'

He stepped out of the tree cover and walked slowly towards the gate. He had almost reached the gate, when it creaked open and out stepped Pandey Sir.

Kabir turned around that very instant and started running back when he heard Pandey Sir call out to him, 'Hey, Kabir!' Kabir froze.

'What are you doing here?' Pandey Sir's voice rang in his ears.

'I ... I ...' He was at a loss for words, when Pandey Sir's words saved him. 'Aaah, jogging,' said Pandey Sir, pointing towards his shoes. 'Nice shoes.' 'Hehe ... hehe ... yes yes ... jogging ... yes ... jogging,' he fumbled in reply.
'Good for health. You carry on,' Pandey Sir said, as he walked off down the narrow path.

The minute Pandey Sir left, realization hit Kabir. 'So this is what it was?' he thought, beginning to run towards Aditya.

'Come, let's go,' he said, when he reached Aditya, and without waiting for him to respond, he started running down the narrow lane to go home.

'Wait, at least tell me what happened,' Aditya cried, running after him.

'I will tell you and Akriti together,' Kabir shouted, as he continued to sprint. Aditya ran behind him.

By the time Aditya reached home, Kabir was already there. He had reached a couple of minutes earlier, and was on Akriti's laptop. Akriti was standing next to him. When she saw Aditya, she threw him a questioning look and asked, 'What happened?'

'I don't know. Ask him,' Aditya replied, trying to catch his breath.

'Guys, come here,' said Kabir, turning the screen with the Google homepage towards them. He spoke as he typed, '15 Private Drive, Solan,' and he looked up at them. 'This is the address we went to today. Where we saw Pandey Sir go in and collect a packet of cash.'

'Packet of cash?!' both Aditya and Akriti exclaimed together.

'Yes, I saw a packet of cash in his hand. The envelope was open and a few notes were peeking out.'

'Damn,' said Aditya. 'What a cheat.'

'Not so soon, Aditya. Things may look different from what they are,' Akriti argued. 'Maybe. Maybe you are right,' said Kabir. 'But then, how do you explain this?' And he pressed the ENTER button on the laptop and tapped the screen. 'This.'

When Aditya and Akriti turned towards the screen, the search results of 15 Private Drive, Solan were on the screen.

'Oh my god!' exclaimed Aditya. Akriti was equally surprised.
The search results indicated that 15 Private Drive was owned by Mr Sibal, the owner of Solan International School.

'Pandey Sir goes to the house of the owner of Solan International School and comes out with a wad of notes. Damn!' Aditya exclaimed. 'That can only mean one thing. He was hand in glove with Solan International to defame Sacred Heart Public School.'

'And what I didn't tell you is that the money was in an envelope which had the SIS logo on it,' Kabir said, and then added sombrely, 'For whatever that's worth.'

CHAPTER 8

It was late in the evening by the time the three
finished discussing the recent developments. Aditya
and Akriti decided to walk Kabir home. His Mom had
offered to send the police jeep as she didn't want him
walking back alone, but Aditya and Akriti wanted to
spend some more time with Kabir and so offered to
drop him back.

They walked along silently, each lost in thought, their
shadows trying to keep up with them as they turned
each bend in the hillside.
Once Kabir was safely home, Aditya and Akriti began

to walk back the way they had come. 'You know Adi, there is something that does not quite add up in our story,' Akriti said. She had pulled out her torch for a short, dark stretch.

'And what does not add up?'

'Why would Pandey Sir try to set fire to the lab to discredit the school, just before the inspection. We believe that Pandey Sir is guilty, because we are assuming that SIS orchestrated this. But why would SIS do this? It is such a cheap thing to do.'

'Yes, it is,' Aditya agreed.

'No school will ask anyone to do something like this. You learn values at school. The teachers cannot end up destroying these values.'

'Well that's what I thought as well, till I saw that front-page advertisement from SIS,' Aditya said. 'Come on!' He waved his hand in front of her face. 'We only fire up imagination. Nothing else. Remember!! Did they leave anything to our imagination?'

Akriti thought for a second as she silently watched a stray dog try to open the lid of a garbage bin. Then she said, 'Pandey Sir should have known better. He should have realized that people would suspect him. And that is what is making me feel that he may not be the guy.'

Suddenly, they saw Mehra Uncle, the local grocery store owner, walking towards them. 'What are you both doing out at this time?' he asked as he came closer. 'We are on our way back after dropping Kabir home,' Aditya replied. Then to avoid any further questions, they wished him and walked away swiftly.

When they were a safe distance from Mehra Uncle, Aditya continued, 'Once someone confronts Pandey Sir, we will know.'
'Who will, is the question,' Akriti responded.

'It has to be Kabir's Dad. Only Police Chief Walia can question Pandey Sir.' Police Chief Walia was one of the most respected citizens of Solan. As crime in the hill station was relatively low, Chief Walia did not have to flex his muscles too much. He could get his work done with love and affection, notwithstanding the impressive handlebar moustache on his diminutive frame. But what mattered most was that Chief Walia was very fond of the SMS gang.

Later that night Kabir texted Aditya and Akriti. 'Dad says that he will come to the school tomorrow and meet Pandey Sir.'

CHAPTER 9

'Bye Mom! Bye Dad!' Aditya and Akriti yelled, as they ran towards the door on their way to the bus stop.

'Wait, wait!' Their Mom hurriedly came after them. 'Say bye to Dadaji also. He is feeling bad that you guys are in your own world and don't even talk to him.'

'Where is he?' Adi asked, slightly irritated.
'Must be in his bedroom reading the newspaper,' Mom replied. 'Last night he was complaining that these days you both don't say bye to him before leaving for school.'

'Why can't he sit in the balcony in the morning and read the newspaper? That way, he can talk to all of us rather than sit alone in his bedroom and read,' Akriti complained as she ran towards the bedroom. 'It would also be easier to say bye to him,' Aditya added.

Their grandfather was hooked to the newspaper and despite failing eyesight, he sat in his room with a magnifying glass and read the newspaper from the first page to the last every morning.

Aditya and Akriti had tried to introduce him to the e-paper version of the *Times of India*, so that he could read it on the iPad. That way he could zoom in and out and increase the font size to read comfortably, rather than struggle with the magnifying glass and the newspaper. But he was not willing to switch to the e-paper. For him the feel of the paper was important.

When the bus reached school, it was already abuzz with excitement. And this was just the start of a very hectic day. Students had been

asked to clean their respective classrooms. The tables were being scrubbed and the blackboards wiped clean with a wet cloth. The children had never seen them so black or so clean! The cleaners, driven by Rehamat Chacha, were wiping the floor repeatedly. The floor shone like a mirror – so clean that you could see your face on the tiles. The children had been prohibited from walking in the corridors, to minimize the area that required to be cleaned again. The atmosphere was festive, and filled with anticipation.

Later that day, when the three were walking back from the lunch room after the break, Kabir said, 'Dad told me last night that sometimes in crimes, the messenger is the culprit. In many of the murder cases that he has solved, the one who comes in to report the murder is often the one who has committed the crime.'

'So? What's your point?' Akriti asked. She was not a big fan of such generalizations.

'He still thinks it is Rehamat Chacha who did something in the lab,' Kabir declared.

'Oh come on!' Akriti disagreed. 'Rehamat Chacha wouldn't hurt a fly. And more importantly he cleared the "look in the eye" test with flying colours.'

'Look in the eye?'

'That day when I met him and asked him about the lab incident, his eyes were crystal clear. As clear as the water of the Solan stream,' she said, pointing towards the back of the school in the direction of the natural stream. 'Had he been guilty, it would have shown.'

'Hmm. Yet Dad is quite sure it is him. I told Dad that some teachers were talking about Rehamat Chacha and Sister Leena having a loud argument a few days back and he said that he will speak to both of them when he comes to school next.'

'You can never become a detective, Kabir,' Aditya said, stepping into the conversation.
'Oh yeah? Really? And says who?'
'Me. To be a detective you often need to go with your gut. You need to have a theory or hypothesis. And once you form a hypothesis, you should go after that till you are convinced it is right or wrong. You are just shuffling all over the place. First you said it was Pandey Sir, now it is Rehamat Chacha. Your gut is horribly wrong.'

'Whatever,' Kabir said, and walked away from the two of them angrily.

'Come on, Adi,' Akriti reprimanded him, making a face. 'Couldn't you have been gentler?'

'As detectives, we should not malign someone unless we have reason to suspect them. Just because he was around the crime scene should not make us ignore the fact that he has served the school for twenty years. Maybe more,' Aditya said.

'Fair. But Kabir is also a friend,' Akriti said. 'Please go after him. Go and pacify him and get him back. And I can see you've really been brushing up on your detective lingo,' she added with a wink. Aditya reluctantly set off down the long school corridor in search of Kabir.

CHAPTER 10

A maths test on a day filled with so much excitement and activity was quite the anti-climax. The Fourth Graders reluctantly put pen to paper and mind to maths in the post-lunch period.

'They should ban maths,' said Kabir in the break between periods.

'You need to practice to get better at it,' Akriti argued. She was a bright student and maths didn't frighten her the way it frightened Kabir.

'You know what maths is?' Kabir asked innocently.
And without waiting for her response, answered,
'Mental Abuse Towards HumanS.' Then he smiled
at his own joke and walked away.

When he returned to the classroom, he looked
sad and downcast. A big frown had replaced the
sunny smile.
'What happened?' Akriti asked him, in a voice
filled with concern. 'And where did you disappear?
We were worried about you.'

'Dad just left,' Kabir replied.

'He had come to school?' Aditya asked.

'Hmm,' Kabir nodded. 'He had come in to speak to
Pandey Sir.'

'That was real quick!'

'Well, yes. He spoke to the principal and they
called in Pandey Sir.'
'And ...?' Akriti asked anxiously.
'And nothing. He spoke to him.'

'You already told us that!!! What happened?' Akriti
asked impatiently.
'Well, before going, he said just one thing – the

SMS gang has got it all wrong. They need to improve a lot before they think of themselves as mystery solvers.'

Instead of explaining anything further, Kabir asked them to meet him in the park right after school.

That afternoon, the three got off the bus close to the twins' home and headed to the park.

Aditya was the first to break the silence. 'You discussed our hypothesis with your Dad? Why didn't you tell us?' he exclaimed. 'And how have we got it wrong?'

'Yes, I did. I wanted to give him a reason to talk to both our suspects when he came to school,' Kabir answered. 'And looks like we did, indeed, get it wrong. Pandey Sir agreed that he did talk about money in the loo, but it was not for what we think it is.'

'Then?' Aditya asked softly, surprised that they hadn't got it right.

'Pandey Sir gives private tuitions. Our school does not permit that. He was worried that someone would hear his conversation and take him to task. That's why he was speaking in a low tone in the toilet. He was talking to someone who had to pay him for those private tuitions. He has even shared the numbers with Dad so he can cross-check.'

'What about the SIS founder's house. And that wad of currency,' Akriti said.
'In the SIS envelope,' Aditya added.
'Well, he was teaching physics to the founder's son. Pandey Sir is the best physics teacher in town. According to Pandey Sir, he couldn't say no to the request from the founder of SIS because that is the only other employment opportunity for him. If something goes wrong for him here, SIS is the only school he can go to. And if he angers the founder of that school, then he is virtually blocking himself here in SHPS for life.'

'But from what you told us, the tone in which he was speaking to the SIS guys from the loo, wasn't particularly courteous. After speaking in that tone, he has some hope of going to that school.'
'Well that's the point. He is not going,' Kabir replied.

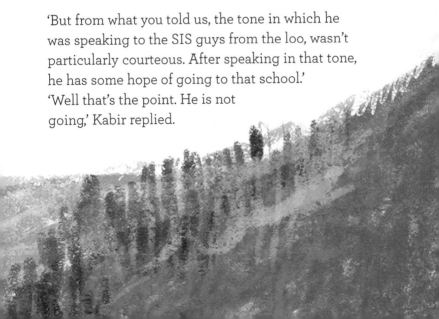

'What?' Akriti exclaimed. 'And what about the declaration he made in school that day?'

'Well, apparently, he was lured by that school. But then he spoke at length to Sister Maria Leena and finally the school managed to make him stay back. He is not going anywhere.'
'If it is not Pandey Sir, then it has to be Rehamat Chacha.' Akriti's face dropped a thousand feet.
'They spoke to him as well.'
'And ...'
'The fight he had with Sister Maria Leena was because Sister Leena wanted him to go to the hospital to care for his son who has malaria. But Rehamat Chacha didn't want to. He was worried about the inspection.'

He didn't want to disappear at such a critical moment for the school.'

'Oh damn! And we suspected him. How mean of us,' Aditya said guiltily.

'Sister Leena yelled at him and told him that if he didn't go, she would sack him.'
'Such a darling he is, Rehamat Chacha.' Akriti was as guilt-stricken as Aditya. 'Well, this teaches us mystery solvers only one thing: we mustn't judge too hastily. Definitely not as the SMS gang.'
'And by the way,' Aditya said, turning angrily towards Kabir, 'the SMS gang did not get it wrong. You did. You were the one who gave us that information about

Rehamat Chacha and Pandey Sir and put us on the wrong track. You are the one who got it wrong.' He then stared hard at Akriti. 'And you tell me not to be rude to this guy!' Saying this, he started walking swiftly across the grass to the other end of the park.

'Hey,' Kabir shrugged his shoulders and looked at Akriti, 'and this is the guy who tells me that I am part of the SMS gang.'

'Of course, you are!' Akriti put her hand around Kabir's shoulders, trying to pacify him. 'I will handle Aditya. You relax.'

Kabir picked up his bag and slowly walked out of the park to go home.

Akriti waved to Aditya, who was now at the far end of the park. 'Let's go home,' she shouted.

The school inspection was on Friday. There was just a day to go.

CHAPTER 11

Grandpa was back in the balcony reading the newspaper by the time the two sleuths returned home. The twins waved to him cheerfully, happy to see him outside. 'I'll be with you in a minute, Dadaji,' Aditya called out as Akriti went off to change out of her school uniform.

Aditya was still seething from his discussion with Kabir, and that irritation showed in his mood. 'There is more light in the balcony in the morning, Dadaji,' he said, flatly, a hint of sarcasm in his voice.
Although Grandpa caught on, he didn't lose his cool.

'Well yes, Adi. But the sun is a bit too strong in the morning. It does not allow me to read with my magnifying glass. That is why I read the newspaper in my bedroom. In the evenings, like now, the balcony is shady, so I am able to sit here.'

Aditya nodded his head, although he didn't quite understand what Grandpa was saying. Akriti too had joined them by then. Aditya looked at her and raised his eyebrows. But Akriti shrugged her shoulders, indicating that she too hadn't understood. Aditya made a mental note to ask his parents why Grandpa had said he didn't like to read in the balcony in the morning.

Soon the sun went down over the distant hills and the town was quickly wrapped up in a grey, fading light. Aditya and Akriti thought this was the perfect place and time for a quick story from their grandfather. Grandpa was an incredible storyteller and could tell a story on demand anytime, anywhere. 'Dadaji, please tell us a ghost story!' they implored their grandfather.

It was dark by the time the twins and their grandfather came back inside. It wasn't cold but the story had given Aditya and Akriti the chills so they both had their arms folded across their chests as they went to their room to lay out their uniforms for the next day. Soon after dinner, Aditya went to the hall and called Kabir on his landline number. Kabir's mother picked up the phone. 'Kabir!' she called out. Aditya could hear Kabir mutter grumpily under his breath as he took the receiver from his mother's hand. 'Oh dear, he's still angry with me,' Aditya said to himself. Then, after mumbling a quick apology, Aditya asked, 'Have the cops got any other information about the fire in the school?'

'Nothing,' Kabir replied. 'Dad says that our principal doesn't want it to become a big issue. She doesn't want anyone to talk about it.'

'Probably she is worried that if the School Inspector gets to know of this, he might not give the school a good rating.'
Akriti had picked up the receiver on the parallel line when she heard

Aditya talking to Kabir. Now she asked, 'Yes. But what about safety? And in any case, it is in the papers. The inspector will know about it.
For sure.'
'I am sure Sister Maria Leena will take care of safety. She is paranoid about it, remember. She wants to keep it low key because she is concerned about the school. She sounded very worried when she was speaking to the Postmaster General. She wants SHPS to be the best school in Solan. Especially this year when she has competition from SIS.'

No one argued with Aditya's defence of Sister Maria Leena. They chatted together for about fifteen minutes and then hung up. Akriti walked up to her Mom's room for her night ritual. Every night before going to bed, she led her Mom back to their bedroom so she

could cuddle up with her and
go to sleep.

Aditya was reading a book that he had
borrowed from the school library when
Akriti and his Mom entered the room.
Akriti shut her eyes and was about to
sleep, when she heard her Mom say,
'Dadaji was upset that you were very
rude to him today.'

Akriti sat up immediately. But she
didn't say anything because Mom was
taking to Aditya. Aditya was taken
aback. 'I did not say anything. I just
told him that there was more light in
the balcony in the morning. That's it.'

'It's not about what you say, Adi.
It is more about how you say it.'
Mom obviously didn't buy Aditya's
argument. 'According to Dadaji, your

tone bordered on ridicule.
That upset him. He complained
to Dad.'
Aditya was upset. 'He could have
told me if he didn't like what I had
said or how I said it. Why tell Dad?
And Akriti and I did spend time with
him this evening. He even told us a
ghost story.'

'It's okay. Be nice to him. He is your
grandfather. He loves you,' Mom said
as she got up and walked to the door.
As she was switching off the light,
she turned towards Aditya, 'Do you
even know why he doesn't sit in the
balcony to read the newspaper in
the morning?'

'He said it was too bright. So?' Aditya sat up on his bed. 'I would imagine, brighter light would mean it would be easier to read. No?' he asked in a shaky voice. When his Mom didn't nod her head in agreement, he gave in, 'OK. Tell me!'
Mom smiled and came back to the bed and sat down. Akriti also left her bed and moved closer to Mom.

'In the morning, the sun rises on the side of our balcony. Our balcony faces the east. So, the sunlight directly hits our house. That's why in the morning, the balcony is quite bright. Dadaji has a problem with his eyesight. He uses a magnifying glass to read the newspaper. You have seen that; he carries it with him all the time.'

Both Akriti and Aditya were completely engrossed in what she was saying.

CHAPTER 12

It was Friday. The day of the inspection was finally here. The whole school was in a festive mood. Everything looked bright and sparkling. The tubelights had been changed, the walls white-washed. Damp spots on the wall had been covered with wallpaper. Windows had been thrown open and curtains drawn aside so the sunlight could stream in and give the school a cheerful look. The children looked their best too. They were all in neat and clean uniforms, some neater than usual. The school day had begun much before time, as the children had been asked to come in half an hour early. The teachers had come even earlier – most had been in school since 6 a.m., to oversee last-minute arrangements. Everyone believed the school was going to score top marks. The inspector was expected to arrive in school at 10.00 a.m.

'Don't you wish school looked like this every day?' Aditya asked Akriti, cheerfully.

'As long as they don't call us early like today, everything else is fine,' Kabir butted into the conversation. Then noticing some commotion on the road outside, he looked out of the classroom window. A few parents, flowers in hand, had gathered on the footpath outside the school. 'Members of the Parent Teacher Association,' Kabir declared. His father was there too, in full police uniform. The sun glinted off his brass buttons as he stood upright in the sun. Actually, Police Chief Walia hadn't wanted to come, but the principal had insisted. She felt that the police chief's presence would make the School Inspector more favourably disposed towards the school.

Suddenly, the sound of people clapping rang through

the school. 'Looks like the inspector has arrived,' Kabir
declared, as he turned towards Aditya and Akriti.
Sister Maria Leena had planned the inspector's visit
down to the last detail. After spending some time with
the principal, the inspector would come up to the third
floor which housed the Fourth and Eighth Grades and
the labs. The entire school knew his schedule.

As the children of the Fourth Grade waited
excitedly in their classroom, Pandey Sir came in.
'He will be here soon,' he announced. 'So everybody
take your seats. No smart-alecky answers. He should
go back impressed.'

Akriti's seat was next to the window which opened out
onto the corridor. She looked out to see if
the School Inspector was on their floor.
At the far end of the corridor she
could see the biology lab. Next
to which was the infamous

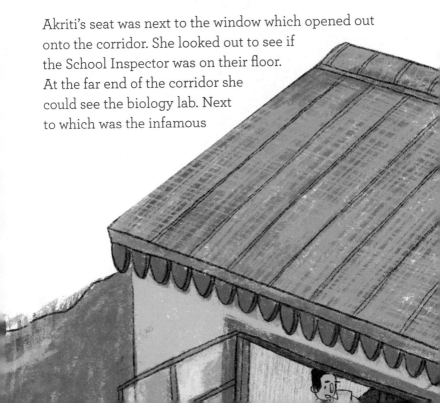

physics lab. The lab looked bright and new. Then she saw Rehamat Chacha rush out of the physics lab and hurriedly disappear into the biology lab.

Before Akriti could make sense of this, they heard the inspector approach along with the principal and some others. She looked out of the window as she saw Sister Maria Leena cross her line of sight, followed by someone she hadn't seen before, but who she guessed

was the School Inspector. Behind him were a few school teachers and finally the PTA members. Kabir's father, Chief Walia looked at her and smiled. Akriti smiled back. As everyone entered the classroom, Akriti happened to glance back into the corridor.

And then she froze.

CHAPTER 13

Within moments all hell broke loose.

It began with Akriti noticing smoke coming out of the physics lab.

'Fire' she whispered, 'it's the physics lab again.' And then realizing that no one had heard her, she yelled, 'Fire! Fire!' and turned towards the main door. 'FIRE IN THE PHYSICS LAB, AGAIN,' she shouted at the top of her voice. As everyone looked at her, their expressions quickly went from shock to alarm.

'Fire?' Inspector Gomez looked perplexed. 'Again?' More than the fire, the word 'again' seemed to have caught his attention. Even if he had meant to ignore the newspaper reports about fire safety in schools, now he couldn't.

The children rushed out of the classroom towards the staircase. This was part of the fire drill they had been taught – leave the school building and move to an open ground. In the melee, someone pushed Sister Maria Leena. As Sister Leena tried to regain her balance she grabbed at the nearest person for support, which, unfortunately, turned out to be Inspector Gomez. The next moment, they both collapsed onto the ground in an untidy heap. Everyone stepped around them and rushed out. Everyone except Aditya, Akriti and Kabir. The three of them ran towards the physics lab.

When the three reached the lab and rushed in, breathless with excitement, who should they find there, but Rehamat Chacha himself.

Kabir came to a sudden stop. When he turned towards Akriti, he had an I-told-you-so look on his face. Rehamat Chacha stood there holding an empty bucket, his starched white pathan suit drenched with water.

'So you did what you wanted to?' Kabir asked accusingly.

'There was no choice. I had to put out the fire,' Rehamat Chacha said, pointing to the bucket he held in his hand. He had not understood Kabir's taunt.

Aditya turned to look down the corridor. Sister Leena, who had recovered by then, was standing outside thundering at the children. 'Down to the open ground. Follow the drill, students,' she yelled. Inspector Gomez, who was standing next to her, seemed confused. He walked towards the physics lab, closely followed by Sister Leena. Then standing at the entrance, he turned and said, 'Sister Leena! When I read about the fire in the newspaper, I thought it was a one-off. Looks like your school has made fire a habit.'
'Yes, we had an incident a few days back. We have checked everything since then. Now it is very safe,' Sister Leena answered, adjusting her habit that had gone askew owing to the fall.

'Then what is this?' the inspector said, as he pointed towards the window, the half-burnt curtains and the ashes on the table. Aditya, who was standing close by, looked at the spot. The apparatus was undisturbed. Just wet from the water that Rehamat Chacha had poured on it.

'Why haven't you filed an incident report with the education department, Sister Leena?' Inspector Gomez asked angrily. Then spotting Police Chief Walia, he asked, 'Has an incident report been filed with the police?'

'We are aware. We investigated it as well, but couldn't find anything. So we decided to close the case,' Chief Walia replied. 'Closed the case!!!' The inspector almost yelled. 'Is this how casually you take the safety of children?' he asked angrily. 'What is the use of imparting good education to children if you can't take care of their safety?'

'That's not the case, Sir,' Sister Maria Leena said, alarm and agitation writ large on her face. But Inspector Gomez would have none of it. 'I am going to write out a report that this school needs to take care of fire safety first and only after that will it be given a license to carry out any teaching

activities. In case it fails to clear the fire safety norms, I am going to recommend that the school shut down and all students be transferred to SIS. We don't want their education to be impacted.
Do we?'

'That's so unfair. Don't you think, Akriti?' Aditya muttered, turning to look at her. But Akriti was not there. 'How is that possible,' he thought, mystified, 'she was standing beside me just a moment ago.' He scanned the growing crowd outside the lab to try to spot her. But saw Kabir instead. 'Where is she?' he gestured to Kabir.

'Sir, I would request you to take a round of the school and check all the facilities and the quality of the students before you take any such step,' the principal pleaded. 'We have been the best school in Solan for years,' she added, her voice trembling with emotion. Aditya hated the inspector now. In his mind, he was hurling abuses at him.

'Do you know why the fire broke out?'
Inspector Gomez asked menacingly.
'We will figure that out. Soon,' Chief Walia
added, quickly stepping in to try to salvage
the situation.

'It's been three days since the last fire. And you haven't figured it out. And now there is this incident again today. You have put the lives of students at risk. They could have died.'

'But, sir, it is a minor incident.'

'Minor? You call this minor?' The inspector raised both his hands towards the skies in exasperation. 'You claim it is minor when you don't know what happened?' He looked around at everyone's sullen faces. 'The day you figure out what went wrong, call me back.' He then began to stomp towards the stairs. There was pin drop silence. Everyone was stunned at this turn of events.

'I think we know what went wrong.'

The voice of a girl voice rang out on the floor. Aditya went pale as he recognized it. Kabir put his hand on Aditya's shoulder and found him shaking with apprehension.

Everyone turned towards the origin of the voice. And then they all saw Akriti standing inside the physics lab.

A stunned Aditya rushed to her side. 'Are you crazy?' he whispered. 'Everyone is looking at you.'

Sister Leena also walked into the lab swiftly. She looked very angry. 'What is going on, Akriti, you need to get out of the lab. NOW!' And when Akriti didn't, she repeated, 'Didn't you hear what I said?'

'But, Sister, I think I know what caused the fire,' Akriti said slowly.

By then, Inspector Gomez had also walked into the room. Sister Leena was furious, yet she had to keep calm, since the inspector was now present there. 'So you know what caused the fire, young lady?' he asked.

'Who are you?'

'My name is Akriti, I am a student of 4th C.'

The School Inspector looked visibly impressed, if not at the intelligence, then most certainly at the confidence of a Fourth Grade student. He didn't know that Akriti was the genius. The brain behind the SMS gang. Police Chief Walia had also walked in by then.

'I think I know,' said Akriti as she walked to the window and looked out. The sun was up in the sky, beaming down in full fury. Half the curtain was burnt. The papers that had been lying on the table had turned to ash. The experiment apparatus on top of the table was wet. Possibly from the water that Rehamat Chacha had thrown on it, to douse the fire.

'Akriti, what are you doing?' Aditya whispered, as he held her elbow and tried to pull her away. 'Come, let's go back to the class. You can be thrown out of school for this,' he added, with a rising sense of panic.

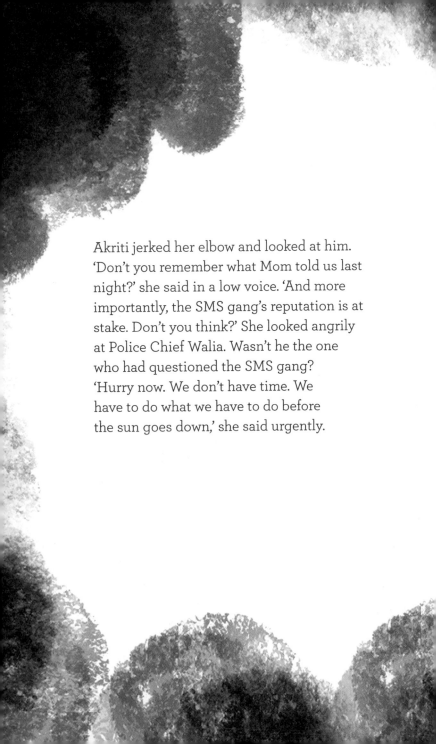

Akriti jerked her elbow and looked at him. 'Don't you remember what Mom told us last night?' she said in a low voice. 'And more importantly, the SMS gang's reputation is at stake. Don't you think?' She looked angrily at Police Chief Walia. Wasn't he the one who had questioned the SMS gang? 'Hurry now. We don't have time. We have to do what we have to do before the sun goes down,' she said urgently.

Aditya snapped into attention when
he heard this.

The very next moment Akriti walked
up to Sister Leena and said, 'I need
five minutes, Sister Leena and Inspector
Gomez Sir.' She paused for effect and then
pointed to the person standing quietly to
one side, bucket in hand, adding, '... and
Rehamat Chacha.'

CHAPTER 14

Five minutes later, Rehamat Chacha opened the door to the laboratory, to let in Sister Maria Leena, the School Inspector and Chief Walia.

'You better have something good to show us,' the School Inspector threatened. He hadn't regained his composure after the fall. Now as a stray bunch of hair fell across his forehead, he pushed the strands back with an impatient sweep of his hand.

Sister Maria Leena appeared to be equally irritated. Only Chief Walia showed concern. As they looked around the room curiously, nothing seemed amiss. The table next to the window had been cleared of ashes. The curtains—or whatever remained of them—had been drawn and the equipment next to the window wiped dry.

'The fire was not an act of sabotage. It was an accident which will never happen again,' Akriti began confidently. 'Accident?' Inspector Gomez asked. 'How can you be so sure?' 'Because of this,' said Akriti as she walked up to the curtains and pulled them back. Sunlight streamed into the room through the big window. Rehamat Chacha moved closer with a bucket of water in hand.

A smiling Aditya handed a few dry newspapers to Akriti, who went close to the window and placed them there, right under the experiment set-up.

Sister Maria Leena's eyes grew round in anticipation. Chief Walia's lips curled upwards in a smile. The inspector continued to wear a stern expression.

'And now let us step back and wait,' Akriti

said with a flourish.

Within a minute, a hole started forming in the newspaper and a couple of seconds later, the paper burst into flames.

'Wow!' Sister Maria Leena exclaimed. 'How did we miss that?'

The School Inspector was awestruck as the flames leapt up menacingly. 'Which class did you say you were in?' he asked Akriti, with a smile.

'4th C, Sir,' Akriti replied.

'How did you know this in 4th C? Isn't that too early to know this scientific fact?' he asked, even as Rehamat Chacha stepped in and poured a bucket of water over

the burning papers to ensure that they didn't cause any further damage.

Aditya moved forward to stand next to Akriti. The police chief smiled and stepped into the conversation. 'So the SMS gang has solved this case for us,' he said.

'Well, Sir,' Akriti said in reply to the School Inspector's question, 'We haven't learnt this in class, yet.'

'Then how did you know?' Inspector Gomez asked.

'When the fire happened for the first time, we had two strong suspects. Rehamat Chacha and Pandey Sir. Rehamat Chacha because he had had an argument with Sister Leena, and Pandey Sir was a suspect as he was moving to SIS. We also overheard him talking to someone about money, that too in whispers. Almost as if he had something to hide.'

'OK,' Inspector Gomez said, getting interested.

'Rehamat Chacha could not be the one for he has always considered this school as his own. He has been here longer than anyone. He would not do anything to bring disrepute to the school. And the argument with Sister Leena was because Rehamat Chacha was too committed to the school inspection, to the extent that he even ignored caring for his hospitalized son. As far as Pandey Sir is concerned, he had quit to go to SIS. So he could have done it to help SIS. But later we realized it was not him.'

'Hmmm,' Inspector Gomez said. He was now all ears. There was complete

silence in the lab as everyone
listened carefully to what
Akriti had to say.

'The fire this morning reminded me of our
grandfather. He reads the newspaper with the help
of a magnifying glass. In the mornings, he sits in his
bedroom and reads the small font of the newspaper
using the lens – the magnifying glass. In the evening,
he sits in the balcony and reads. Mom explained this
to us last night. She told us that in the morning the
sun shines directly on the balcony, so Dadaji is unable
to sit in the balcony and read.

Mom told us that when the sun's rays fall on a lens, or the magnifying glass that Dadaji uses, the lens focusses the rays on a point on the paper. And the focussing of the sun's rays at a point produces a great amount of heat at that point ... enough to burn the paper. That's why Dadaji does not risk reading the paper in the balcony in the morning. In the evening, the rays of the sun do not fall directly on the balcony and hence they don't focus on the newspaper and create heat.'

'This morning,' Aditya continued his sister's story, 'when Akriti saw the place where the fire accident had happened, she found that the physics equipment that had been placed near the window had a lens. The lens was positioned in such a way that the light rays from the window focussed on the paper below, generating the heat that caused the fire. This happens only during a particular time of the day when the sun shines in strongly through the window and the lens turns it into a deadly weapon of fire.'

'Very intelligent,' Inspector Gomez said. 'But I need to understand one thing. If such were the case, why didn't it happen earlier. Why now?'

'Because normally the equipment is kept inside the lab, away from the window. However, there was a leak in a water pipe close to where the equipment originally lay, so Pandey Sir had asked Rehamat Chacha to move the equipment to a different place. As luck would have it, Rehamat Chacha moved it closer to the window. The risk of the sun's rays falling directly on the lens and causing a fire was never there earlier. The equipment has been lying there for the last four days. The first time it caused a fire was when Rehamat Chacha pulled open the curtains in the morning, to let in the sunlight so that the damp patches could

dry out fast. Even today, Rehamat
Chacha opened the curtains because
he wanted the room to be brightly lit
when you walked in, Inspector Sir.
The open curtains let the sun's rays in
directly and these hit the lens, causing
the papers kept near the equipment to
catch fire.'

The School Inspector smiled. 'It is
amazing how a student of Class 4 has
solved a problem which even you guys
couldn't solve,' he said looking directly
at Police Chief Walia.
'These guys are gifted,' the Chief
smiled. 'They are intelligent brats who
know how to put their knowledge to
good use. No wonder they are called the
SMS gang,' he added proudly.

'SMS?' The inspector had no clue what
this was or what it stood for.
'Super Mystery Solvers,' Akriti hastened
to answer.

'Ah. That's wonderful. You deserve that tag.'
'Do we still have to go to SIS?' Kabir asked the School Inspector. Chief Walia reached out and pinched Kabir playfully. The sarcasm had not been missed.

A visibly happy inspector smiled and looked at Sister Maria Leena. 'Well, no. Why would I do that to a school that has such fabulous students? In fact, I might even consider asking the students at SIS to join your school, if I don't find them up to the mark. What do you think about that?' And he winked at Kabir.

'Thank you, Sir.' Akriti said. 'We are happy that we have been able to solve the mystery of the lab on fire. We don't want to compare ourselves with the students at SIS. We are happy where we are. I am sure they are too.'
Sister Maria Leena walked up to Akriti and hugged her. 'Thank you, my love,' she whispered into her ear.

'You might have just saved the school from humiliation. Thank you.'

The School Inspector left three hours later, singing praises of the school, the students and the principal. It was no surprise that the school came out on top in the district inspections. A result which Sister Maria Leena would continue to brag about for the next year. Pandey Sir stayed on in the same school and didn't join SIS.

Aditya's admiration of Akriti went up manifold after the case was solved. Though Aditya credited Akriti with solving the case, he didn't lose an opportunity to remind her that they got to know about the specific property of magnifying glasses only because he asked the right questions. Akriti only made use of the answers their Mom gave them.

CHAPTER 15

Akriti and Aditya were rewarded with a sleuth room of their own in the basement of their house. A room that would later become the Headquarters of the SMS gang. Entry to the basement room was restricted with only the twins allowed in, along with Kabir, of course. Aditya and Akriti brought down some small pieces of furniture to set up the room: the beanbag from their room, a small side table from the hall, an old rug and some cushions that Mom no longer wanted.

A week after the fire incident the three met for their first formal meeting. It was at this meeting that they decided the password for entering their headquarters. After some heated and not so heated discussions, they decided on 'I-T-I-T-Y-A-B-I-R' with the last three letters of each of their names.

Once they had sealed the logo they created a badge to proudly display it. They also made detective note-keeping diaries from the unused pages in their old notebooks and drew up an important Code of Detective Conduct.

It was Sunday morning, ten days since the school inspection and fire incident. Aditya and Akriti were in their basement office writing the rules of conduct on a chart paper, when there was a knock on the door.

'Password,' Akriti called out.

'It's Mom,' their Mom said in reply. Akriti ran to open the door. Mom walked in along with Kabir who was closely followed by a man in uniform. 'What was Chief Walia doing at their house, that too at this hour?' Akriti wondered.

Aditya jumped off his beanbag and rushed to the door. He fist-bumped Kabir and smiled at Chief Walia, bowing his head in respect. 'You might be wondering why I am here,'

☐ We shall **Knock twice** before giving out the password to enter the basement office.

☐ We will always keep the password secret and **NEVER** write it down anywhere.

☐ We will carry our Detective badge with us AT ALL TIMES.

☐ WE WILL NEVER GIVE UP!

Chief Walia began. 'A cricket match between India and Australia is going to be played in Solan. As a reward for solving the mystery of the school on fire, I am going to get the SMS gang passes to the match. Pavilion passes,' he said. Adding after a pause, 'Right next to where the players' room is. But for now, get ready. We are all going for breakfast to Hotel Hilltop. I need to go there to make sure that it is in shape and ready to host the cricketers for a longish weekend.'

'Yaaaaay! Uncle Walia, you are awesome,' said Aditya as he jumped up and hugged Chief Walia.

'From now on you guys are not the Super Mystery Solvers, you are the SMS Detective Agency. And you will help the Solan law enforcers. We were wondering if the SMS Detective Agency could help us resolve whichever case we are struggling to get to the bottom of.'

Aditya looked at Akriti, who was listening very carefully to every word Chief Walia was saying.

'With your permission,' Chief Walia looked at Mom before he continued, 'I would like to engage the services of this brilliant bunch of kids. Hope they will be happy working with us.' 'Of course, we will,' yelled Akriti and Aditya together, drowning out their Mom's feeble voice of protest. Mom, quite naturally, was only worried about the safety of the kids. As far as the SMS gang was concerned, she was very proud that they had solved the mystery of the school on fire. Not just her, Dad and Grandpa were equally proud. In fact, when Akriti and Aditya related the whole story to their parents, Grandpa joked that his magnifying glass had played an important role too.

'Of course, we will,' Kabir said happily. Akriti walked up to him and hugged him fondly. Aditya came forward and did the same. 'Well, as Uncle Walia just said, we are now not ONLY the Super Mystery Solvers or the SMS gang ...

WE ARE THE SMS DETECTIVE AGENCY.'

THE SMS
DETECTIVE AGENCY

LOOK OUT
FOR OUR NEXT
MYSTERY:
THE
MYSTERY
OF THE
MISSING
CAT!

ABOUT THE AUTHOR

Ravi Subramanian is the award-winning author of nine novels. His stories are set against the backdrop of the financial services industry. He has won the Economist Crossword Book Award for three years in a row, as well as the Golden Quill Readers' Choice Award. This is Ravi's first fiction series for children. Visit him at www.ravisubramanian.in

ABOUT THE ILLUSTRATORS

Ayeshe Sadr & Ishaan Dasgupta work together out of their small studio currently in New Delhi, India. A textile designer and a graphic designer respectively, Ayeshe and Ishaan found a common love for illustration and created 211 Studio in 2009. Through the years they have worked on a wide variety of illustration projects, ranging from children's books, food packaging,

wedding cards to restaurant murals. They find inspiration in mythology, fine art, textiles and nature and try to incorporate those elements into their work. When not working or spending time with their two cats, they love travelling and cooking.